E SUS
Sussman, Scott.
Otto grows down

DATE DUE

AVON PUBLIC LIBRARY
BOX 977/200 BENCHMARK RD.
AVON, CO 81620

EAGLE VALLEY LIBRARY DISTRICT

1 06 0004835874

P9-DFQ-312

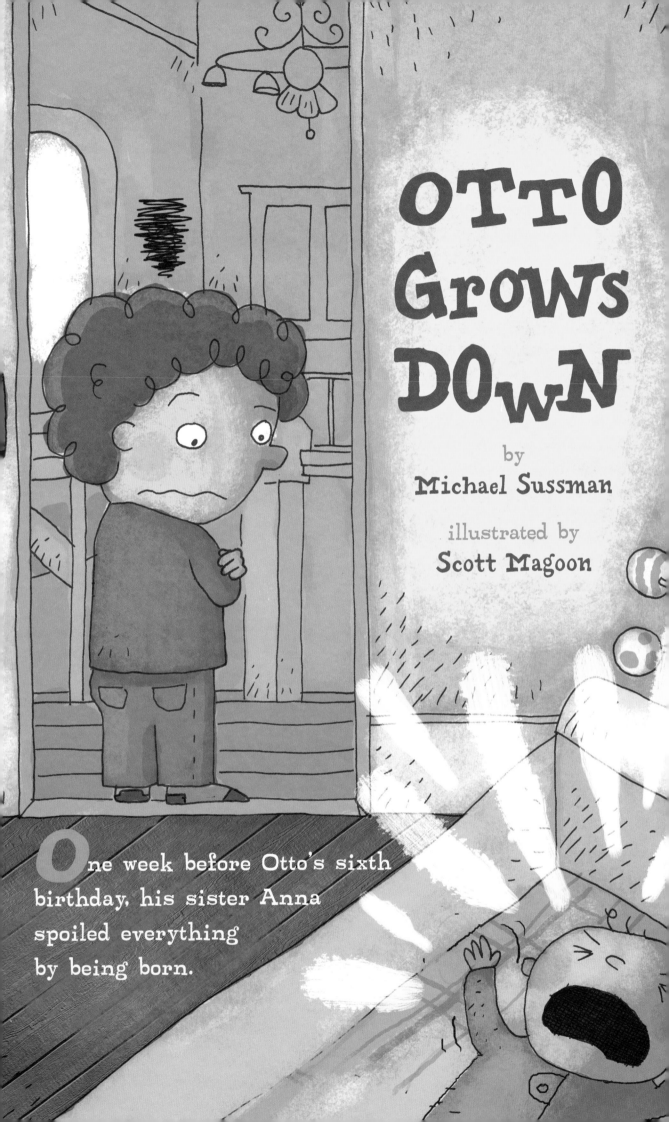

OTTO GROWS DOWN

by

Michael Sussman

illustrated by

Scott Magoon

One week before Otto's sixth birthday, his sister Anna spoiled everything by being born.

Even at Otto's own birthday party,
Anna got all the attention.

As Otto took a giant breath to blow out
his birthday candles, Anna started
crying. Otto's mom pushed
a rattle into his hands.

"Shake it for Anna," she said.
JONG JINGLY!
⠀⠀⠀⠀⠀⠀⠀JINGLY JONG!
That sound! It was Otto's old rattle—
the one that sounded like underwater
bells. *I love this rattle,* Otto thought.
Why does Anna get to have it?

"Come on, Otto," said his dad. "Make a wish!"
I'll make a wish, all right! thought Otto,
as he shook the rattle with
all his might.

I WiSH AnNa was NEVeR bOrN!

Then a strange thing happened.

The candles lit up again.

Was it a joke?
Did his dad use trick candles?

Otto noticed his new birthday watch.
The second hand was ticking in the wrong direction.

When Otto started rewrapping his presents
and giving them back to his friends,

he really knew something
crazy was happening.

Time was going backwards!

Friday, at kindergarten, everything was backwards too. First it was mess-up time and everyone took toys from the shelves and scattered them all over the room.

In Art, Otto wiped the paint off a perfectly good painting, leaving a blank sheet of paper.

At recess, Otto couldn't get used to sliding *up* the slide.

By the time it was morning and his dad picked him up, Otto just wanted to spit out his breakfast and go straight to bed.

Each day brought a new surprise. On Thursday, Otto's mother put their dinner in bags and delivered it to the supermarket. On Wednesday, the barber made Otto's hair longer.

Tuesday was trash day,
and Otto helped bring in the garbage.

And on Monday, Otto's parents returned Anna to the hospital. Time really *was* going backwards! Otto's wish had come true. No more rattle-swiping, birthday-wrecking baby sister.

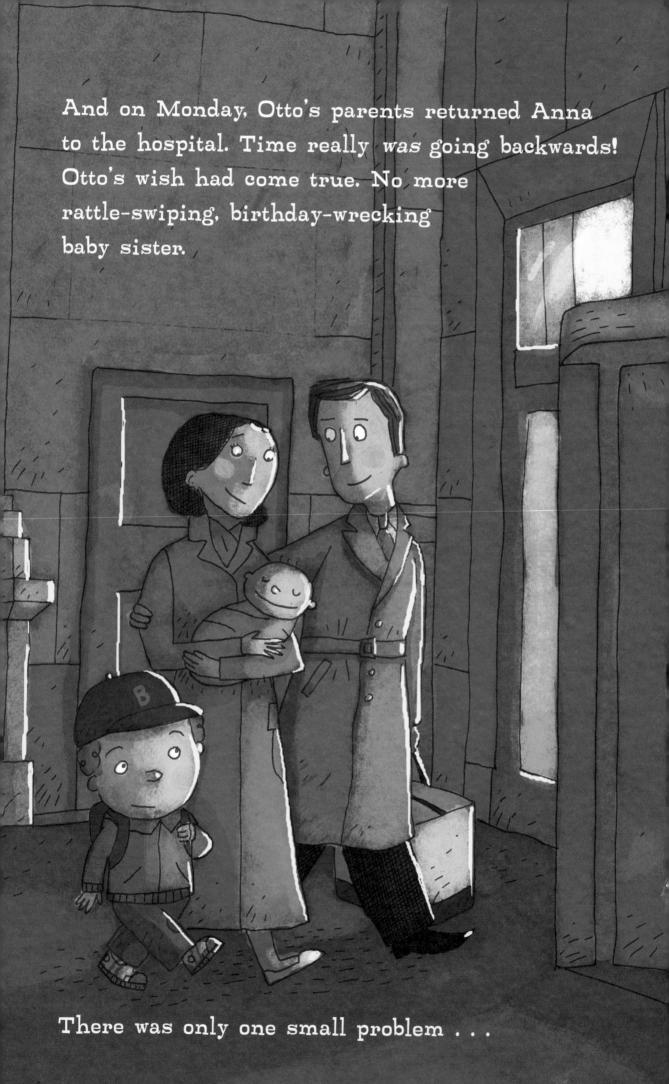

There was only one small problem . . .

St. TEMPUS HOSPITAL
MAIN ENTRANCE

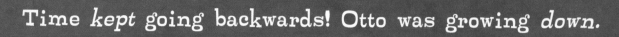

Time *kept* going backwards! Otto was growing *down*.

On his fifth birthday, he watched his friends spoon cake out of their mouths and onto their plates. They handed them to Otto's mom, who arranged the slices together and stuck five burnt-out candle stubs on top. Otto sucked in. The candles lit up. He shut his eyes and thought,

I
WiSH
I wAs
SiX
aGAiN!

AVON PUBLIC LIBRARY
BOX 977/200 BENCHMARK RD.
AVON, CO 81620

When he opened his eyes,
nothing had changed.
Otto was five, and time was
still going backwards.

Otto took baths when he
was clean—and they made
him dirty.

And going to the bathroom
was downright disgusting.

Wonderful things *did* happen, though.
One summer day, a van arrived
and Otto's best friend Bob moved
back to the neighborhood.

But at night, lying awake,
Otto felt bad about Anna.

Each year at his birthday party, Otto tried to fix
the wish, but as time passed he knew fewer
and fewer words. On his fourth birthday, after
playing pull-the-tail-off-the-donkey, Otto wished,

TiMe
tURN
aROuNd!

But it didn't work. On his third birthday,
Otto wondered whether this was all a bad dream.
He pinched himself and wished,

Me
WaKE
uP!

It didn't work.

On his second birthday, he wished,

OttO BiG!

But Otto didn't get big.
He grew smaller and smaller and soon
had to wear ridiculous baby outfits.

Then, one horrible day, his mother put
him in a diaper.

Otto realized that if he didn't think of something
soon, he'd disappear like his sister. There was one
last chance: Otto's first birthday.

At the party, Otto's mom made him wear a bib with yellow bunnies. Everyone spoke baby-talk to him, and when they talked to each other, he couldn't understand a word. Without words how would he make a wish?

Never had he felt so alone.
Otto's first birthday would be
his last. He would never grow up.

And then he heard it:

JONG JINGLY! JINGLY JONG!

That sound! It was his rattle!
Otto snatched it from his mother's hand.

He sucked in and the candle burst into flames.
Otto shut his eyes, shook the rattle . . .

JONG JINGLY!
JINGLY JONG!

. . . and wished with all his heart.

When Otto opened his eyes, he had blown out six candles. Otto's mom sliced the birthday cake and handed out the plates, just like normal.

Chocolate cake never
tasted so good.
Otto blinked.
It felt great to be six again.

Otto went over to Anna lying in her crib. Anna cooed at him. Otto paused, handed her the rattle, and smiled. "I'd rather grow up with Anna," said Otto, "than grow down without her."

For Ollie—
up, down, or sideways . . . —M.S.

For Zach and Ethan.
I couldn't have wished for better brothers—S.M.

STERLING and the distinctive Sterling logo
are registered trademarks of Sterling Publishing Co., Inc.

LIBRARY OF CONGRESS CATALOGING-IN-PUBLICATION DATA

SUSSMAN, MICHAEL B.
OTTO GROWS DOWN / BY MICHAEL SUSSMAN ; ILLUSTRATED BY SCOTT MAGOON.
P. CM.
SUMMARY: WHEN TIME GOES BACKWARDS, GRANTING SIX-YEAR-OLD OTTO HIS WISH THAT HIS ATTENTION-
STEALING BABY SISTER WAS NEVER BORN, IT KEEPS GOING BACKWARDS, AND
OTTO FINDS HIMSELF GETTING YOUNGER AND YOUNGER.
ISBN 978-1-4027-4703-8
[1. WISHES--FICTION. 2. TIME--FICTION. 3. GROWTH--FICTION. 4. BABIES--FICTION.
5. BROTHERS AND SISTERS--FICTION.] I. MAGOON, SCOTT, ILL. II. TITLE.
PZ7.S96568OT 2009
[E]--DC22

2008028229

10   9   8   7   6   5   4   3   2   1

Published by Sterling Publishing Co., Inc.
387 Park Avenue South, New York, NY 10016
Text © 2009 by Michael Sussman
Illustrations © 2009 by Scott Magoon
Designed by Lauren Rille
Distributed in Canada by Sterling Publishing
℅ Canadian Manda Group, 165 Dufferin Street
Toronto, Ontario, Canada M6K 3H6
Distributed in the United Kingdom by GMC Distribution Services
Castle Place, 166 High Street, Lewes, East Sussex, England BN7 1XU
Distributed in Australia by Capricorn Link (Australia) Pty. Ltd.
P.O. Box 704, Windsor, NSW 2756, Australia

Printed in China
All rights reserved

Sterling ISBN 978-1-4027-4703-8

For information about custom editions, special sales, premium and corporate purchases,
please contact Sterling Special Sales Department at 800-805-5489 or specialsales@sterlingpublishing.com.

AVON PUBLIC LIBRARY
BOX 977/200 BENCHMARK RD.
AVON, CO 81620

STERLING

New York / London

AVON PUBLIC LIBRARY
BOX 977/200 BENCHMARK RD.
AVON, CO 81620